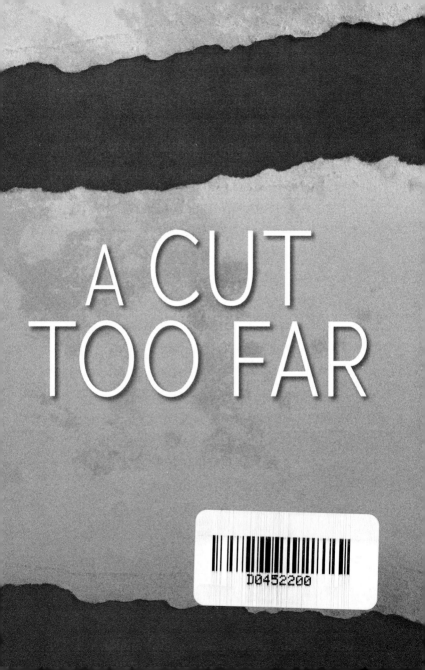

A CUT TOO FAR

SUSPENDED

A CUT TOO FAR

Herman Brown

MINNEAPOLIS

Darby Creek
A division of Lerner Publishing Group, Inc.
241 First Avenue North
Minneapolis, MN 55401 USA

For reading levels and more information, look up this title at
www.lernerbooks.com.

Front cover: © Charles Knox Photo Inc./Dreamstime.com (teen guy); Cover and interior: © iStockphoto.com/Sorapop (ripped paper).

Main body text set in Janson Text LT Std 12/17.5.
Typeface provided by Adobe Systems.

Library of Congress Cataloging-in-Publication Data

Brown, Herman, 1971–
        A cut too far / Herman Brown.
            pages cm. — (Suspended)
        Summary: Chace has been bullied for years by Ivan, first for his facial deformity and then for his mother's Iranian-American boyfriend, but when he decides to pay back Ivan's Internet attacks with a cyberthreat of his own, he faces suspension from school—and worse.
        ISBN 978-1-4677-5709-6 (lb : alk. paper) — ISBN 978-1-4677-8096-4 (pb : alk. paper) — ISBN 978-1-4677-8824-3 (eb pdf)
        [1. Bullying—Fiction. 2. Racism—Fiction. 3. Abnormalities, Human—Fiction. 4. Cyberbullying—Fiction. 5. Conduct of life—Fiction. 6. High schools—Fiction. 7. Schools—Fiction.] I. Title.
PZ7.B81383Cut 2015
[Fic]—dc23   2014040602

Manufactured in the United States of America
1 – SB – 7/15/15

CHAPTER ONE

I leaned all my weight on the handle of the shovel and pried a blue, football-sized rock out of the dirt. With my gloved hands, I hoisted it into the back of the pickup truck. It banged and tumbled in the bed with the others.

That's when the cough of a chain saw started to travel down the slope about fifty feet away. Tahir pulled the throttle cord three times in quick succession, and the engine caught. The saw added to all the other rattling sounds: the rocks I dropped, the brush cutter Mom was running through the sumac, and the Stooges wailing on my earbuds. All that and the buzz of anger in my head.

Besides the Stooges song, which I was not about to turn off, there was nothing I could do about any of it. I'd made my bed, as Mom said. I wished I *was* in bed. As for the anger, that had been roaring through my brain like a dive-bombing Stuka for weeks.

I felt a little dizzy.

Tahir pulled his goggles down and drove the chain saw into the tree on the lakeside. Wood chips flew all over, and sawdust spat back onto his face. He pulled the saw out and started another cut at a downward angle. After a few seconds, he kicked a wedge out of the trunk.

He walked around to the uphill side of the tree and pushed the chain saw into the trunk on the side opposite the wedge. In a few seconds, the two-story pine tree made a splitting sound and leaned toward the water. It tilted slowly at first, then faster, landing with its tip in the lake.

Tahir went right away to the next tree. This one was an aspen, a really nice-looking one. I sat down in the shade of the truck and shut my eyes. At least I had the Stooges to keep out the real world.

I dare you to try to take a break with my mom around. You can't do it. After about ten seconds, she noticed I wasn't picking up rocks. So she cut the motor on the brush cutter and came over from the other side of the driveway. I could feel her standing in front of me, but I kept my eyes shut and the music going.

Finally, she plucked out one of my earbuds.

"What's going on?" she said.

"I have a headache."

She looked down at me for a few seconds, trying to figure out if I was lying. All my life I've gotten these terrible headaches. It has to do with my deformity. Mom doesn't call it that, a *deformity*. Neither does Dad, for that matter. But plenty of people use the word. Sometimes I do, sometimes I don't, depending on how it's making me feel at the time.

The deformity of which I speak is my jaw. It's huge. It sits on the bottom of my face like the prow of a canoe. I have a gross underbite and very crooked bottom teeth, creating intense pressure that runs through my jaw and skull. I've been wearing some serious industrial-strength braces for a few years now, which doesn't do anything to relieve the pressure, let me tell you. Sometimes it's unbearable.

I guess Mom decided I was full of it, because she said, "Get up. It's work time, not lounging time. You can have a headache later."

I opened my eyes. Sweat dampened her temples and the collar of her green T-shirt. Her mouth formed a hard line. Behind her, the sky was pure blue. The sun ignited the treetops so they glowed green. If I hadn't been so angry and didn't have such a headache, I might have thought it was a beautiful day.

Since I got called to the principal's office

last week, I'd had a hard time appreciating nice things like great weather or tasty food. I'd been angry at the world, and Mom had been nonstop angry at me. That's why I was up north in Otter Tail County clearing land for Tahir instead of being back at school in Minneapolis.

Ms. Robb had suspended me for the week. Mom had flipped her lid. She said there was no way I was going to sit around the house listening to music and playing strategy games online, so she made me come up here to work for Tahir. He was going to build a lake home this summer, but first, he had to get all the sumac, poison ivy, trees, and rocks out of the way. The tractors would come in next week and dig the hole for the foundation.

In a way, it was actually Mom's fault that all this happened in the first place. Her and Tahir's. I say *in a way* because I know I am responsible for my actions. And I didn't *tell* Mom it was her fault. No way. She wouldn't buy it, for one thing—I made my bed, etc. And plus, I'd never tell her what was at the root of my actions. I'm just saying, I *could* argue that I'd been defending her and Tahir.

Not that I was a big supporter of Tahir. I'd rather that Mom had stayed with Dad, that nothing had changed at home, and that Ella and I still had a regular set of parents. But if your mom has to have a boyfriend, Tahir was fine. Or he should have been fine. Except as soon as he came into my life, things pretty much went to hell.

For the vast majority of my school life, this kid Ivan has teased me for the obvious reason: my jaw. He called me Chace the Face, which is just pitiful. I mean, that's all he could come up with? You've got the world's largest jaw to make fun of, and you come up with Chace the Face? This was one bully who wasn't truly devoted to his craft. An embarrassment to bullykind. I got pretty good at ignoring him and his sidekick, Toua, and I even kind of felt sorry for them sometimes. Kind of. In another year, I'd be out of high school and never have to see them again—except when they changed my oil at the Quick Lube or something. But when Ivan found out my mom was dating an Iranian American, it was like he found his bullying bonus points. All he'd been missing all these years was a little racism! In his tiny little mind, anyone from the Middle East was a Muslim terrorist. Eventually, I snapped.

Well, I didn't "snap," exactly. But I got back at him, and it felt good. Even after getting suspended, I didn't regret it. Even after prying rocks out of the hard-packed earth, I didn't regret it. He deserved what he got, even if I was paying for it with a week of forest removal. Stomping around in the mud and, because it was Minnesota, the first mosquitoes of the year too. Swatting bugs and breaking my back to clear land for somebody else's lake house.

Anyway, it looked like Mom was going to make me work through the pain, so I got up.

The chain saw was making a different noise now. I looked over, and Tahir was walking through a bunch of saplings. He sliced through them like whiskers. *Rrrrt, rrrrt, rrrrt.*

I must have looked unsteady on my feet, because Mom sighed. "Take a break, I guess."

"Thanks, Mom."

"Just don't laze around too long. You're not out here to enjoy the scenery."

Believe me, I thought. *I'm not enjoying anything.*

CHAPTER TWO

Dad moved out of the house near the end of last summer. He and Mom said they agreed to separate, but from what I've read online, it's almost always one member of the couple who drives the separation. This was Dad's idea, I was sure. He'd been cranky for, like, a year, always barking at Mom and me and my little sister, Ella. He started finding ways to stay out of the house. Going to happy hour after work or going to Twins games with friends without even stopping home. He started taking weekend trips alone.

Or maybe he wasn't alone. He might already have been seeing this woman, Meg.

Pretty much as soon as he moved out, he began to talk about her when Ella and I visited. And it was only a few weeks before he wanted us to meet her. She came over to his apartment and made us all a spaghetti dinner. She was nice, but I didn't feel good about her being with Dad. It felt like one of my headaches had settled in my stomach. Dad wanted us to like her so bad, but all I could do was think about Mom and how she'd been dropped for this lady.

Mom didn't date anyone. We spent a lot of time together, me and her and Ella. All of a sudden we were the ones going to Twins games, taking bike rides, seeing free concerts at the lake, and finding all kinds of other stuff to do together. I guess we needed things to talk about and think about that weren't the divorce. Or maybe Mom just wanted us to be happy. I started to think of her as a victim, like the divorce had happened *to* her, not *with* her.

Then she brought Tahir home. This was a day in March. When I got home from school, he was sitting on the couch, talking with Ella. She was in middle school and got home about twenty minutes before me. Tahir had given her a really nice catcher's mitt, which she needed because her old one was too small and she was planning to try out for the high school team. Ella was a really great catcher, and I knew she'd at least make JV. But she looked really uncomfortable sitting there with that mitt and Tahir smiling all goofy.

When I got my boots off and hung up my jacket and scarf, Mom introduced us. "Chace, I want you to meet Tahir." As we shook hands, I watched to see if he'd flinch when he saw my jaw, but he didn't so much as glance at it. He just smiled with that goofy expression.

He had a gift for me too: an owner's manual for Supermarine Spitfires, the legendary fighter planes used by the British during World War II. Since I'm a World War II nut and an aspiring engineer, my heart may have fluttered a little at that moment.

But only for a moment, because I slowly realized that Mom was introducing me to her boyfriend. I got that headache-in-my-stomach feeling.

Tahir made dinner for us that night. It must be written down in some divorced-parent's guidebook. *When introducing your kids to a new boyfriend or girlfriend, have the new partner cook dinner.*

Tahir prepared this Iranian food that was very different from any food Ella or I had ever eaten before. There was some weird-tasting lamb stew on rice, and on the side he served some flatbread called naan. I actually liked everything and cleared my whole plate, but Ella had about one-and-a-half bites of stew and then just ate the bread. Tahir tried to get her to talk about softball. She just nodded or shook her head or gave the shortest possible answers: yes, no, I don't know.

"Chace," Mom said. "Tell Tahir about your engineering club trip."

"We're going to the university for a geothermal energy presentation," I said. "Then we're going to the lock and dam."

"Oh?" said Tahir. He had a bushy black mustache that scrunched up like an inchworm when he chewed his food.

"Yep," I said.

"Tell him about it," Mom said.

"What do you want to know?" I said. "This professor is going to give a presentation, and then we go to St. Anthony Falls. That's about it."

"Sounds amazing," Tahir said. Somehow I'd never thought of the trip as "amazing."

"Yeah," I said.

"They're going to learn the history of the area and all about the Army Corp of Engineers," she said to Tahir.

"Oh!" he said, sitting up straighter. "That sounds amazing!"

"I need to do homework," I said. "Can I be excused?"

Mom looked a little deflated, but she let me go.

"Me too?" Ella said.

"Of course," Mom said. "Just clear your dishes, okay?"

We brought our dishes to the dishwasher and got out of there as fast as we could. When I took a last glance at Mom and Tahir, their expressions were changing quickly. The frustration about us kids left their eyes, like they were pleased to suddenly find themselves alone together.

That was a lot to think about, but I forgot all about them in about ten seconds once I started reading my new vintage owner's manual.

* * *

A few weeks later, Mom brought Tahir to my basketball game. I'm a fairly big kid, so I play center, but I'm not very athletic, so I've been a second stringer for all of high school. That meant I was on the sideline most of the game and there wasn't much for Tahir to see. I got some minutes toward the end, though, since we were up big.

At one point I blocked a shot, came up with the ball in the scrum that followed, and passed it downcourt to our point guard, a guy named Ollie Sadusky. Ollie passed it off quick to Ivan, the shooting guard, and he scored. I don't mind saying I felt pretty good about setting up that play, even though the other team mostly had their second stringers in by that time too.

After the game, Mom and Tahir came over to congratulate me on the win. Mom hugged me, and Tahir raised his hand to high-five. I obliged him, but we sort of missed and just brushed fingertips. Standing nearby, Ivan, my lifelong personal bully, guffawed as he took off his headband. Like, super funny, right? It was just one more uncomfortable moment with my mom's boyfriend, the guy who desperately wanted me to like him. But Ivan apparently thought it was the most hilarious thing ever.

"Great game," Tahir said to me. "You *denied* that guy!" He meant my blocked shot, which suddenly seemed embarrassing instead of awesome. It's not like I didn't like Tahir or I didn't want him to say nice things about me. It's just that it seemed weird, this guy coming around all of a sudden and acting like we were buddies. My mom's boyfriend.

To make things even more awkward, Ivan laughed again, as if Tahir was this huge dork who knew nothing about basketball. Which is actually untrue. Tahir knows quite a bit about the sport. He had been asking for weeks to come to a game. It was a goofy comment for him to make, sure, but he was looking for anything to say to make me like him. Anyway, after Ivan basically laughed in his face, we all sort of stood there in silence like we were waiting for him to apologize.

Maybe I should have said something, like, "Take a hike, Ivan." But I didn't. Finally, Tahir just smiled at Ivan and said, "Good game," and we left. But the next day at school, Ivan sat next to me in health class.

"So that's your mom's new boyfriend?"

Ivan was a tall, skinny kid with oily hair who wore button-down Oxford shirts all the time. He looked like a Wall Street inside trader, complete with the dark eyes that suggested he was up every night completing sleazy deals. He was rangy and quick, which made him pretty good at basketball as well as flicking me on the ear from across the aisle in class.

"What are you talking about?" I said.

"Abdul, at the game last night. I'm surprised he came—aren't sports against their religion or something?"

"You're an idiot," I said.

"If she marries him, do you have to convert to terrorism?" he said.

His buddy Toua set his books down on the desk next to Ivan. "What's up?" he said to Ivan.

"Just talking to the Face. His mom's in love with an Arab."

"He's Iranian," I said.

"*He's Iranian*," Ivan replied.

Toua laughed. He was Hmong, so I thought

he might be more sensitive about racist jokes. We had a lot of Hmong kids and Somalian kids at our school, and they took a lot of bullying. It got pretty bad sometimes. But apparently Ivan's comments didn't bother Toua. "Don't get on any airplanes with him," he said.

Just then Mr. Giovanni walked in, and I yelled out, "Ow!" and rubbed my arm.

"What's going on here?" Mr. Giovanni asked.

"Nothing," Ivan said, acting confused.

"Nothing except you punched me in the arm," I said. Ivan had been tossed from class a couple times in the past few weeks, and I knew he was on a short leash. I figured it wouldn't take much to get him kicked out of class.

I was right.

"Ivan, go see Ms. Robb," Mr. Giovanni said. Ivan glared at me, but he picked up his stuff without saying anything and left the room. I just smiled at him.

"Now then," Mr. Giovanni said. "Any other interruptions or can we get started?"

CHAPTER THREE

Two days after I got Ivan booted from health class, I received an e-mail welcoming me to my new membership at a Middle East-themed adult site. It was graphic. I deleted it, but that night, I got two more e-mails. I tried to log into the site so I could discontinue the membership. After contacting the webmaster and getting a password reminder sent my way, I succeeded, but it was too late. I was on all kinds of spam lists. I started getting nasty e-mails constantly.

I suspected that Ivan had signed me up, but I wasn't sure until the next week in health class. He and Toua sat behind me and giggled for the whole class. When I glanced back, Ivan showed me a drawing of a naked guy with a turban. I was pretty shocked, and I must have looked it, because they started cracking up.

After lunch, the drawing was taped to my locker but with an addition. There was a shorter guy with a huge jaw, also naked, with his arms around the guy in the turban.

I tore it down and crumpled it. A couple girls with lockers nearby were laughing.

"What's that all about?" asked Ollie, whose locker was next to mine. Our families had been close when we were younger. Since both sets of parents had divorced, the families never saw each other anymore, and Ollie and I had little in common besides basketball. In spite of all that, we'd remained good friends.

Ollie was handsome, for that matter, while I was the freak with the big jaw. Girls liked him, and not just "as a friend." He actually knew some things about sex, whereas I knew little more than what I'd seen in the e-mails I'd gotten.

"Nothing," I said.

"Don't let those guys bug you," he said.

"Easy for you to say."

"I know but still."

I threw the balled-up paper into my backpack and loaded my books on top of it. Ollie was still watching me, and something crossed my mind. "Did you see them put it up here?" I asked.

He nodded.

"Why didn't you stop them?"

"I don't know. I guess I thought it was kind of funny."

"Well, it wasn't."

He laughed, then he stopped.

"You're supposed to be my friend," I said.

"I know," he said. "Sorry."

* * *

That afternoon when I got home, Tahir and Mom were getting ready to go to a movie. Tahir had put his jacket on, but Mom was running around looking for her earrings and barking at Ella about when to take the lasagna out of the oven. Even though Mom was flustered, she looked excited. Happy. I realized that I hadn't seen Mom and Dad have fun together in years. It was nice to see Mom doing something enjoyable now, even if seeing her with another man still made me uncomfortable.

"Hey, Tahir," I said, tossing my backpack on the couch, but then I picked it up again, as if Tahir might grab it and rifle through it. The offensive drawing was inside.

"Hey, Chace!" he said. He took his hat off and gave me a big smile.

"Are you an Arab?" I asked. I'd been thinking about it all day. I had corrected Ivan when he called Tahir an Arab, but I didn't actually know if Tahir was an Arab or not. I was pretty sure a person could be Iranian and Arab at the same time.

"I'm not," he said.

I thought about that a second. "What *is* an Arab?" I asked. Ella lifted her eyes from the book she was reading to follow the conversation.

Tahir explained that it's an ethnicity. Originally Arabs were people from the Arabian Peninsula, but now *Arab* applies to anyone who speaks Arabic and comes from the Middle East or northern Africa. I asked him if Arabs are Muslims.

"Most Arabs are Muslim," he said, "but *Arab* doesn't mean 'Muslim.' Some Arabs are Christian."

Tahir told me that his family was Persian. They fled Iran in 1978, when he was eight, to escape before a revolution. They packed as many of their things as they could in a few suitcases. "We just left the rest behind," he said. "Our books. Our furniture. Most of my toys. Not to mention our friends."

It sounded horrible. But I guess the family made a smart move, because when Ayatollah Khomeini came to power in 1979, Iran became more restrictive. Tahir's family was one of the lucky ones that had enough wealth to get out of the country and start a new life in the US.

"We now consider ourselves Americans," he said.

As he finished up, Mom came into the room, pushing in her earrings. She picked up her jacket and hat and looked to see if we were done. I could tell that she didn't want to interrupt me and Tahir now that we were actually talking, but she also really wanted to be on time to the movie. Tahir finally gave her a love-struck smile.

"We're going to be late," Mom whispered.

"Right, we better go," Tahir said. "Thanks for the talk," he said to me, putting his stocking cap back on. It had a little pom-pom on top that made him look a little bit like a kid, even though he had that big mustache.

"Sure," I said, though I wasn't sure what he was thanking me for.

. . .

"How's Daddy Terrorist?" Ivan called. We were in gym class. Ivan was playing second base in indoor kickball. I was standing on first base after kicking a single.

I ignored him and watched the pitcher roll the ball toward home plate. The kicker let it pass and then threw it back. I had to stand by Ivan for at least one more pitch.

"Hey, I'm talking to you!" Ivan said. I still ignored him, but he repeated himself, and the pitcher laughed. So did Toua, who was playing shortstop.

"What's your problem?" I finally said. The gym teachers, Mr. Cole and Mr. Stoddard, were busy talking in the bleachers.

"What's my problem? I have lots. One is your face. I've been looking at that massive block of ugly for too many years. Another one is Muslim terrorists. And now every time I see your face, I think about how you have one in your house."

Just then the kicker blasted a line drive that sailed over Ivan's head. Ivan turned to face the outfield, waiting for the ball to come back in.

"You're ignorant," I said as I ran toward second. When Ivan got the ball from the outfielder, he turned with it and pegged me in the face with all he had, even though I was standing safely on second base. I hit the floor.

A couple people ran over to see if I was okay. I lay flat for a few seconds. My jaw stung. My head pounded with pain and humiliation.

"That's the third out," I heard Toua say. He and Ivan started jogging toward the bench area.

"He was safe!" someone argued. "Besides, that was a head shot. That's against the rules."

"It was an accident!" Ivan protested. A crowd gathered, and Mr. Stoddard came over. He wore sweatpants and a whistle around his thick neck, just like he did every day of his life.

"What's going on here?" he asked.

"I accidentally hit Chace the Face," Ivan said, smirking. "I mean, I accidentally hit Chace *in* the face. He was ducking to dodge the throw."

"No, I wasn't!" I said, rubbing my jaw. "I was standing on the base!"

"Well, I'm sorry I hit you in the face," Ivan said. "Hard to avoid that. But still, you were definitely out."

Toua nodded to Mr. Stoddard. "He was."

Mr. Stoddard hooked his thumb in the air, the signal for "you're out." And that was that. As Toua and Ivan and the rest of their team started running toward home to kick, I got so mad that I kicked Ivan's leg as he passed, and he fell to the floor. He popped up with his fist balled up and lunged at me, but Mr. Stoddard jumped in front of him.

"Cool it, Rusnak," he said, his hand on Ivan's chest.

"He tripped me!" Ivan said.

"It was an accident," I said. Mr. Stoddard looked me over as if he could judge my sincerity just by the look on my face. When he turned away, I winked at Ivan.

"Play ball," Mr. Stoddard said.

As Ivan backed across the infield toward the home plate area, he pointed a finger at me. "You're going to regret that, Face."

CHAPTER FOUR

When Mom got home from work that night, she knocked on my bedroom door before she even changed out of her work clothes. She did usability testing on websites for nonprofits, and she spent a lot of time working at home in her office. But sometimes she dressed up and went somewhere for a meeting. She didn't like that part, though, and she usually changed back into casual clothes as soon as she could. When she poked her head in the doorway, still wearing a collared blouse and a blazer, I knew she had something on her mind.

I was lying on the bed reading a book about

Operation Torch, a World War II battle in which British and American forces invaded French North Africa to clear out Axis forces there. It was the first time in the war that the US used an airborne attack as a major part of an operation, and Supermarine Spitfires were a big part of the invasion. I had the MC5 coming out of my speakers. About the only thing I loved as much as engineering and fighter planes was early punk rock.

"We need to talk," Mom said.

I put down the book. "What's up?"

"I was looking something up on your computer yesterday, and I saw some things in your search history."

"And?"

She reached over to my iPod dock and turned the volume all the way down. I hated it when people did that—turn it down instead of turning it off. Then you lose your place in the song.

"I know you've been looking at porn," she said.

"No, Mom, I haven't. That was . . ." But I didn't know how to explain it.

Mom looked like she was in pain. Like someone had hit her in the head with a kickball. And I remembered that the site was super racist.

"Mom, Ivan joined me up for this website. I didn't have anything to do with it."

"Ivan," Mom said.

"Yeah, he's been a real jerk lately."

"Ivan," she said again. Like she couldn't believe I was trying to pass off my dirty habits on someone else.

"He's been . . . ," I said again. But there was nothing to say. She already had it in her head that I was a racist sleazeball. Nothing I said was going to change what she saw on my computer.

She chewed her lip, and then it was like she couldn't look at me anymore. She just stared out the window, her eyes getting wet.

"Mom," I tried again. "Please don't worry. It's not what you think."

She nodded, but she still didn't say anything. At dinner that night, she said, "You can have your computer after school for one hour to do homework, but other than that, I will keep it in my room for the next two weeks."

Ella was sitting right there at the table with us.

"Why?" Ella asked.

That was my question too. Why did Ivan choose to torment me? Why did Mom and Dad have to divorce? And why did Mom have to date some guy who made me more of a target? And, good lord, why did we have to talk about this in front of Ella? My sister would never let this go until she got to the bottom of it.

"Nothing," I said.

Mom said, "I'm just sorry your dad isn't around to help with this."

"You mean to punish me?" I asked.

"Seriously, what happened?" Ella said.

"Nothing," I said again.

"Mom didn't take your computer away for *nothing*."

"Not to punish you," Mom said. "To talk with you. To *help* you. It would be nice to have a father around for this situation, that's all I mean."

"What about Tahir?" I said, standing up. "He's practically living here anyway. The way you've been acting with him, I'm surprised you didn't already tell him to give me a father-son chat."

As I left the room, I heard Ella asking Mom again why she took my computer away, but Mom told her to mind her own business.

I went to my room, got my computer, set it on Mom's bed, and went back to my room. I got undressed and climbed under the covers and shut my eyes. It was barely even dusk outside, but I was asleep in a few minutes.

* * *

The next day, I had basketball practice. Mom told me at breakfast that Tahir was going to pick me up. I asked if she could pick me up instead.

"I can't, honey. I have a meeting. Tahir is excited to show up early and catch the end of practice. It will be nice for you two to have some time together. He told me he plans to treat you to Dairy Queen."

"Big deal," I said, carrying my cereal bowl to the sink. Ella paused over her cereal to watch us like a hawk.

"Excuse me?" Mom said.

"Nothing," I said.

"You better be nice to him, Chace. He has done nothing but treat you like a prince."

"Sorry. I just meant, I have plans after practice. With friends. I don't need a ride. Can you tell him?"

She looked at me a long couple seconds, and then she let out a big sigh. "I'll tell him," she said.

"What plans?" Ella asked. "You don't have plans."

"I get it," Mom said and walked out of the room. A second later, the back door slammed shut.

Ella took a big spoonful of cereal. "Nice job, dummy," she said with her mouth full.

* * *

That day at lunch, I got a notice on my phone that I'd been mentioned on Instagram. An anonymous user, whose account had only been opened yesterday, posted a photo of me in the school hallway that morning. The caption read, *Coming soon: A list to make @SpitfireChace feel better. Get ready!* And a bunch of people had already liked it. As I looked at the post on my phone, two more likes got added on. I scanned the cafeteria—lots of people were on phones, but nobody seemed to be looking at me.

I showed the post to Ollie. "Check this out," I said. "What the . . . hell?"

He looked at my phone for a second and handed it back.

"You're right," he said, taking a bite of his salami sandwich. "It's not a very good picture of you."

"That's not the point," I said. "And you know it."

Ollie grinned with one side of his mouth, which was supposed to make him look charming and let me know that he was just joking around. I slapped my phone on the table.

"I'm serious," I said. A couple kids at the table looked at me with *Dude, chill out* expressions.

"I know, I know," Ollie said. "It is weird."

"What do you think it means?"

"I don't know," he said. "But I'm guessing we'll find out."

It didn't take long. About fifteen minutes later, as I walked toward STEM class, my phone buzzed again. I paused outside the

classroom door and let other kids go in as
I checked my phone. Sure enough, it was
another Instragram notice from the anonymous user. This one was a photo of a car with
the caption:

*We usually think about how big Chace's face is.
But it's not bigger than everything in the world.
We think it would be nice to point out a few things
that Chace's massive cinder block of a jaw is NOT
bigger than. We'll be counting down from ten to
the NUMBER ONE THING that Chace's face
is not bigger than. Be sure to LIKE and tell your
friends!*
   10. A Honda hatchback.

Like I did in the cafeteria, I scanned
the faces in the hallway to see if anyone was
looking at me. Seemingly everyone I saw was
laughing into their phones. One of the likes
on this photo was a girl who had a locker by
me and Ollie, a girl named Christa, who I saw

passing by. I grabbed her arm.

"Christa," I said.

"Hey, Chace!"

I showed her my phone. "What's the deal with the list stuff?"

"I don't know! It's totally bizarre!"

She was the kind of girl who spoke with lots of exclamation points in her voice.

"Well, why did you *like* it if you don't know?"

"I don't know!" She looked up at the clock on the wall and slipped back into the crowd. "Gotta go!" she called back.

When I entered the classroom, I sat by myself in a back corner and unloaded my notebook and folder from my backpack. I felt a buzz on my phone in my pocket, but I ignored it. A couple guys from the team reached for their phones at the same time, but Ms. Kaat walked into the room and told them to put them away.

The rest of the day was just like that. My

phone kept buzzing, and I kept resisting the urge to check it. And everyone around me seemed to have their noses glued to their phones—more than usual, I mean.

. . .

When I got home after practice, I went to my room and checked my phone. I had a bunch of Instagram notices and a few texts too. I checked Instagram first. Nine of the ten promised list items had been posted. I was tagged on each one. Here's the list (and the photos):

10. *A Honda hatchback (a Honda hatchback)*

9. *Mr. Giovanni's ego (a picture of Mr. Giovanni from the school website)*

8. *The Stanley Cup (the Stanley Cup)*

7. *1,000 large marshmallows (a huge pile of marshmallows)*

6. *Yoda (a screen shot from* Empire Strikes Back*)*

5. *A goose (a goose floating on a lake)*

4. Those old fighter planes he likes (a Spitfire blueprint)

3. Russia (a map)

2. A box that contains all the delusions of all the Muslim terrorist fantasies about all the virgins that are waiting for them in the afterlife (one of those big storage pods that people park in front of their house when they're moving)

An acidy feeling began to bubble in my stomach. As I stared at the picture of the box with the stupid cartoon on the side, the feeling spread from my stomach to my whole body. It made me want to smash my fist through a wall or scream. It was like the world was this overgrown jungle of hate and cruelty, and you couldn't get away from it. It crowded you in on all sides.

There seemed to be nothing I could do.

If I commented on the pictures, I'd only invite more ridicule. If I said anything to Ivan, he'd deny having anything to do with it.

When I thought about it, I didn't know what made me so angry. Ivan had given me a hard time for years. Why should this be any different? I guessed part of it had to do with the medium. With Instagram, his insults could reach a lot of people. About fifty people had liked each of the items on the list already.

But there was another reason I was so mad. Even though I didn't like the idea of my mom being with another man and even though I wasn't exactly buddies with Tahir or anything, Ivan's focus on the Muslim thing seemed really personal. Invasive. It's like he was in my family's house, in our private lives, cutting us up.

I started to wonder what the number one picture on the list would be, but then I got a pretty good idea. Knowing Ivan, he wouldn't be able to resist saying something about how great he is. Or else it would be something vulgar. And then it hit me.

I checked my text messages. I had three. One of them was from this kid on the team named Darren asking if I'd seen the "hilarious" Instagram photos. Thanks a lot, Darren. One was from Mom, telling me that she'd be home late tonight—she was going to see Tahir after her meeting. The other was from Ollie: *Ha ha ha*. And he attached a photo he'd taken of Ivan in the locker room, just in his jockstrap. Basketball had ended, and baseball was in early practices. I laughed a little bit and felt a little better. Then I laughed harder. Pretty soon I was curled over on my bed, laughing so hard I was crying.

I texted Ollie back: *I know what will be number one on his list. Guarantee it.*

When I got the alert after dinner that night, I was almost excited to check Instagram. I opened the app and sure enough: *And the number one thing that Chace's face is NOT bigger than . . . my junk!*

Thankfully, the photo was just a drawing.

A few seconds later, I got a text from Ollie: *LOL. You called it.*

* * *

The next morning at school, as I was unloading my backpack at my locker, Ollie came up with an idea. *The* idea—the one that would eventually get me suspended. He spun the dial on his locker with one hand and ran his fingers through his hair with the other.

"I think you should get him back," he said.

"How's that?"

He wiggled his eyebrows.

"How's that?" I repeated.

"We have some options," Ollie said. "We could trace that user and report him for harassment. That's one idea. Anyway, come over after school and we'll cook something up."

Ollie was not only a great athlete, great with girls, and popular among all cliques. He was also a stud with computers.

"You don't have to help me," I said. "I'll figure it out."

"Suit yourself," he said. "But I wouldn't mind taking him down a couple pegs myself."

"Ivan?"

Ollie wiggled his eyebrows again, slammed his locker, belched, and started walking away.

"Hey," I said, and Ollie stopped. "I'll come over. I wouldn't mind taking him down either."

"Meet me here after school," he said.

"Okay," I said.

"Oh, and see if you can get a couple covert pictures of Ivan on your phone. I'll do the same."

"Thank you," I said. After the previous day, when it felt like everyone in the school was looking at me and laughing, I was grateful to have a friend.

CHAPTER FIVE

We didn't have practice that day, so after school, I walked with Ollie to his place, a few blocks off campus. His dad wasn't home yet. Neither was his older brother, Arthur. So Ollie grabbed us a couple cans of root beer, and we went to his family's office and turned on the computer. He hooked up his phone to a computer cable, and a few seconds later, we were looking at several photos Ollie had taken of Ivan—including the jockstrap photo.

"We should make sure he made the list first," I said.

"It's him," Ollie said.

"Just be sure."

Ollie logged onto Instagram and brought up the user details for @chacingface, the account that had posted the list. The bio information only said, *Getting our jaw-lies as we pay tribute to everyone's favorite man(dibble)*, but Ollie was able to bring up the IP address linked to the account. He was able to trace that to Ivan's home address.

"Boom," Ollie said.

"Boom," I said.

"Satisfied?" he asked.

"Satisfied. Let's get him."

"What does he have against you, anyway?"

"I don't know," I said. "He's been cutting me down since fifth grade. Just cutting me down, over and over. It's just habit by now, I guess."

"It must be more than that." While we talked, Ollie cooked up a fake account, @ivansucks, and loaded up the jockstrap photo as the profile pic.

"It's like we're pretty close to each other on the social hierarchy, so he tries to push me down to build himself up," I said. "But no matter what he does, he never gets any higher."

"That's because he's a jerk," Ollie said. "What do you want to say in the bio?"

"I don't know. Do you think we can get in trouble?"

"Don't worry about that. Unlike Ivan, I know how to cover my tracks."

"What's his biggest fear?" I asked.

"People finding out he's a huge weenie?"

"People know that."

"People talking about it, then," Ollie said. "We could do this interactive style. Invite people to contribute ideas. Throw a few sock puppet accounts on there . . . it would be pretty hilarious."

"I like it," I said. "Let's see. How about: The home of the 'Ivan is a weenie' movement."

"Good start. But it would really burn if he thought this movement had been going on a long time, and this is only the new home—the digital home. You know?"

"Yeah! Okay, so how about this? 'At last— "Ivan is a weenie" moves to social media.'"

Ollie nodded as he typed. "Awesome," he said. Then he added another line to the bio: *Hashtag your photos of Ivan being a weenie with #ivanisaweenie—and tag us!*

I quick made a new sock puppet account on my phone and uploaded a photo I'd taken of Ivan scratching his nose. I wrote a caption asserting that he was picking his nose, tagged it *#ivanisaweenie*, copied the @ivansucks account, and uploaded it.

"Oh, this is too much fun," Ollie said. He made up another account and liked the nose-picking photo. We spent the next hour adding new accounts and new photos and cross-liking everything. Finally, when we had a good base established, we tagged some real people we knew—and Ivan.

CHAPTER SIX

The next day at school, I used my smartphone to snap another couple photos of Ivan in the hall when he wasn't looking. I chuckled when I checked them on my screen—I was having a lot of fun getting back at him. And I noticed him checking his phone many times that day, which I figured meant he was monitoring the #ivanisaweenie movement.

I also noticed a lot of other kids checking out the photos on Instagram. Between classes I saw Christa, the girl who liked all the "bigger than Chace's face" items, at her locker. "Have you seen these photos on Instagram?" I asked her. I showed her a photo someone had posted of Ivan in front of school this morning. It wasn't a very weenie-ish photo, but the user had tagged it #ivanisaweenie and written a caption: *Getting ready for another day of weenieness.*

"I know!" she said. "It's so mean!"

"What?" I said. "He *is* a weenie. I think it's funny."

She squinted her mouth like she'd just eaten a lemon wedge. "I guess."

"You liked all the list items about my face. What's the difference?"

"No difference!" she said. "I felt bad about that, and so I unliked them all! Did you notice?"

"No."

"Well, I did! Anyway, whoever made the weenie account, I think it's mean." She looked at me with arched brows, as if she knew it was me. Then she glanced down the hall and spotted a couple of her friends. "Well, gotta go!"

Was it that obvious that I had made the account?

Ivan teased me in health class, as usual, but he didn't give it as much effort as usual. He just shot a spitball at me, and he missed. When I looked at him, he didn't even laugh. He seemed to look right through me. I smiled pleasantly.

After baseball practice, Ollie and I went to his house to make some more sock puppets and throw a few more photos up. We had been working for about an hour when his dad knocked on the door and said dinner was ready. Ollie minimized the screen right before his dad popped his head in the room and invited me to stay and eat.

Tahir was eating at my house that night, and the thought of another night with him made me tired. I wanted to skip another super-uncomfortable conversation with the man who was taking over my mom's life and desperately trying to make me and Ella like him. But that wasn't the only reason I felt tired. I kind of blamed him for the "Chace's face" list too.

Even though only one item from the list was about terrorism (and thus about Tahir), I knew that Ivan made the list because of Tahir. And for the last few days, every time I saw Tahir, all I could think about was how all my problems had blown up because of him. Part of me really resented him—not only for taking my mom but also for being Iranian. If he had been from somewhere else, none of this would be happening.

But I felt guilty for feeling that way too. So I had this big toxic mix of crappy feelings. Bottom line, though: I really didn't want to go home and see Tahir. I would just end up feeling worse.

"Sure," I said to Ollie's dad, Jon. "Thanks."

As I sat at the kitchen table, Jon asked me what I like on my chili. He had chopped onions, shredded cheese, sour cream, fresh jalapenos, and crumpled-up saltines. He and

Ollie dumped everything on top of their bowls, so I did the same.

"How's your dad doing?" Jon asked. He pulled a string of melted cheese off his chin.

I used to see Jon and his wife, Sue, quite a lot when I was a kid. They were really close with my parents, but when Jon and Sue divorced, my parents drifted apart from both of them. I guess choosing sides or pretending everything was the same made my mom and dad too uncomfortable. Or my parents didn't want to hide their disappointment that Jon and Sue had wrecked a really great friendship. Soon, Sue moved back to Nebraska to be near her own family. Ollie had wanted to stay in school here, so he lived with his dad.

Now my parents were divorced too. When Jon asked about Dad, I started thinking how cool it would be if he and Jon started hanging out again. The four of us—Jon and Dad, Ollie and me—could go camping or watch football or do other guy stuff together.

"My dad's good, I guess," I told Jon. "I haven't talked to him in a while."

"Oh, why not?"

"I don't know," I said, which was true. I was supposed to stay with my dad last weekend, but I went to a Timberwolves game Friday night with Ollie and a couple other guys instead. "I should go see him this weekend."

"Tell him I said hi," Jon said.

"I will," I said. "But you should call him. I bet he'd love to hear from you."

Before Jon could say anything more, I felt my mouth catch fire and I spit a glob of chili back into my bowl. I started sucking cool air in and out of my mouth as fast as I could.

"Sorry," I said. "That was rude." I drank a full glass of milk.

"No problem," Jon said, "You have to be careful with those hollies." Jalapenos, he meant. "You gotta know what you're getting yourself into."

I scraped the hollies out of my bowl and

set them on a napkin. Then I ate the rest of my chili, which was delicious, and after dinner Ollie and I checked into our Instagram project. It was really blowing up. Dozens of people had liked a photo that one of Ollie's puppet accounts posted of Ivan eating lunch. A guy named Charlie, a skater from school, added a comment: *God, why isn't he dead yet?*

. . .

Things were pretty quiet the next day at school. People still giggled about the "Ivan is a weenie" movement, but Ivan didn't seem as bothered as he had the day before. Baseball practice that afternoon was in the gym since there was a storm going on. Ivan and I got paired up for a pepper drill, and he was totally chill. We actually had a good workout.

Tahir and Mom picked me up after practice, and I didn't mind too much. I felt really bad for blowing off dinner last night, and I'd decided I would try to be nicer to Tahir. So when they came to get me, I made a point of talking to him a little more than usual. Ella was there too, and we all went out to dinner at this gourmet burger place.

That night when I got home, I listened to some Dead Kennedys and read a little history about Stuka dive-bombers. I also thought about what Christa had said about the whole Instagram thing being mean. Maybe she was right, but it bothered me that she'd act like I was the one responsible. I *was* responsible, but she didn't know that. What gave her the right to cast judgment on me?

Just before clicking off the light for the night, I checked Instagram once more. Someone had tagged @ivansucks in a new photo. It was a picture of me—and my mom, Ella, and Tahir after practice. My mom and Ella were talking to each other. Tahir was laughing and had his arm on my shoulder. It wasn't a good picture of him.

But that wasn't the problem. The image

had been made into an FBI wanted poster. At the bottom, it said: *TERROR ALERT LEVEL RED. THIS FAMILY WANTS TO SEND YOU TO ALLAH.*

The user who posted the photo was the same user who had posted the list about my face: @chacingface. As if I needed any more proof, this made it obvious that the user was Ivan, the one guy obsessed with Tahir. My face burned with rage. Seeing my mom up there made it too much. He'd gone too far.

I couldn't sleep that night. I couldn't stop thinking about Ivan taking that photo after practice. Ivan putting my family on the Internet. Ivan smirking to himself as he made the poster. When I shut my eyes, all I saw was Ivan.

The next day, I went to Ollie's house again. Mom still had my computer, so I had to use Ollie's. I took the photo of Ivan scratching his nose and imported it onto his computer. Then I Photoshopped his weaselly face onto a picture

I found on a cheesy heavy metal band's website. Ivan appeared to be cutting his own neck.

I put some flames behind him. Near the bottom of the photo, I pasted in some cheesy blood splatters from a Halloween costume site and added the comment, *Ivan, YOU'RE DEAD*. In a comment below that, I wrote, *We know everything about you*, along with his address, e-mail address, and phone number.

* * *

The next day was Saturday, so I didn't get to see Ivan's reaction. I did see my photo get about sixty likes on Instagram. People had added a few comments like *yeah kill him* and *dead ivan is a good ivan*. Nobody posted any new photos with the #ivanisaweenie tag, though. Everything seemed to die out except for the likes and comments on the *Ivan, YOU'RE DEAD* photo.

When Monday finally rolled around, Ivan looked like an even bigger weenie than usual. His dark-ringed eyes seemed to be full of fear when he looked at me, as if he really thought I was going to kill him. Or maybe I was just imagining things. In gym class, he barely participated in volleyball. He just moped through the motions and missed easy shots. His teammates yelled at him, but he didn't care.

He skipped baseball practice altogether.

That night, as Ella watched some reality show on TV, I laid around on the couch. I wasn't really watching, just thinking about the school day. I had the Sex Pistols cranking on my earbuds. After a while, I brought up the new Instagram account on my phone. Which I still had, even though Mom hadn't returned my computer. I guess the punishment was more symbolic than practical. If I wanted to—which I didn't—I could still access all the porn I wanted.

Anyway, I was surprised that Ivan had acted so weird at school. The photo we put up was pretty corny. It was meant to make Ivan mad, not scared. So I looked at the photo again and tried to see it through his eyes. I guessed if someone had shared a photo threatening me, I might feel differently.

Just then, Mom and Tahir came in the room. They'd been taking a walk in the neighborhood. I shoved the phone between the couch cushions and removed one earbud.

"Hey, buddy," Tahir said.

Buddy now?

"Hey, Tahir," I said. And then I got up and went to my room.

CHAPTER SEVEN

I was in my room, reading on my bed, when I overheard Mom in her room. She was talking on her phone. My ears pricked up because she used her surprised voice. I could only pick up parts of the discussion—she was mostly listening, anyway. But I heard her say, "I've had his computer for over a week."

I thought it was weird that my mom would be talking to someone about my computer, but it didn't occur to me that there was any reason to worry. The whole Instagram war was all kid stuff. I didn't think any adults would intervene. Adults hadn't intervened in all the years Ivan had teased me. They hadn't intervened when he punched me on the arm more than twenty times in math class, when I just sat there and let him because I didn't know what else to do. They hadn't intervened when he'd wiped a big booger on my face in health class and everyone laughed their butts off. Why would adults intervene now?

Whatever the call was about, Mom didn't come into my room to ask about it, and I didn't come out. I figured it would blow over.

Still, the next day at school, I had a bad feeling in my stomach. Something seemed weird about that phone call. Sure enough, I had barely sat down in first period geometry when Ms. Robb came into the room—with a police officer.

"Sorry to disturb your class, Ms. Small," Ms. Robb said. "We need to talk with Chace."

"Of course," Ms. Robb said, looking at me with disappointment.

When I got into the hall, the officer, a

woman with a ponytail coming down her back, stopped me before we walked anywhere. She introduced herself as Officer Bartlett and asked me to face the lockers. I was stunned. I was sure I was going to jail. She told me to put my arms out, and she patted me down all over. Her hands were strong and firm. Then she turned me around by the shoulder. "Just need to make sure you don't have any weapons," she said.

The three of us went to Ms. Robb's office. I walked down the hall as if in a dream. I'd never been in much trouble before. To be honest, I still wasn't sure what I had done. I really felt like the Instagram stuff was just a joke. Harmless. Plus, all of the uploading and tagging took place outside of school, so Ms. Robb couldn't do anything about it. Not her business.

When we got to Ms. Robb's office, it was already occupied. Ivan hunched in a corner next to his mom, this lady who I always thought looked so mean. She had a scowl on her face at all times. That and pasty skin. And her eyes were dark-ringed pools, just like Ivan's. She gave me a look like poison.

The cop stood next to me in the other corner, and Ms. Robb sat at her desk.

"Chace," Ms. Robb began.

"What's going on?" I asked.

"Well," she said, "Ivan has brought a very serious threat to my attention." She turned her laptop around and showed me the photo I'd made of Ivan stabbing himself.

I looked at it a few seconds, as if reading it for the first time. "Wow," I said.

Ms. Robb said, "Ivan has also made a very serious accusation. He believes *you* made this photo."

Ivan stared at the floor, hands in pockets, his sky-blue Oxford shirt untucked at one side. His mom was gripping his arm as if to hold him up.

"He does?" I said.

"Isn't that right, Ivan?" said Ms. Robb.

Ivan's mom jerked his arm. He looked up at me, but he couldn't hold my eye for very long.

"Answer her," his mom said.

"Yes," he said. He looked miserable.

I may have been guilty, but I just couldn't believe that after all these years of being bullied, *I* was the one who would get in trouble.

"Really, Ivan?" I said. "You've been treating me like garbage for years, but the first time someone gives you a dose of your own medicine, you call the cops? You're pathetic."

"Take it easy," Ms. Robb said.

"Mr. Anderson," Officer Bartlett said. "Mr. Rusnak has already given a statement. I'm just going to ask you right up front: Did you put this photo up?"

"What are his reasons for naming me? I'd like to know," I said.

"Just answer my question, please," Officer Bartlett said.

I folded my arms.

"We *will* find out," she said. "You'll make it easier on yourself if you tell the truth now."

I felt something knotting in my stomach, and I realized it had been there for weeks. Anger.

Ever since Ivan started in with the anti-Muslim stuff, he was not only cutting me down, he was cutting down Tahir, who didn't even know. And he was cutting down my mom.

I realized I really did want to hurt him. I didn't want to *kill* him, but I wanted to hurt him. Bad. He didn't deserve to get away with all the stuff he'd said and done. I felt my face get hot, just like it did when I saw that photo of my family. That anger was knotting throughout my body, from the pit of my stomach to the muscles of my big, huge jaw.

"Here's the truth," I said. "Ivan is a racist jerk. He has been bullying me for years, and he has been saying racist things about my mom's boyfriend. He trips me, hits me with balls in gym class, laughs at me, draws dirty pictures about me."

"This doesn't answer the question," Officer Bartlett said.

"Ivan has *tortured* me for so long, but I have lived with it peacefully. And then the other day he put a photo of my family on Instagram and called us terrorists."

"Chace!" Ms. Robb said. "Answer the officer's question. Now."

Tears gathered in my eyes—humiliating. But oh, well. I was too far down this road. Humiliation was a small part of my troubles.

"Yes," I said. "Yeah, I did it. I hate Ivan. But it wasn't a threat. I would never kill anyone. Not even him."

"I believe you wouldn't," Ms. Robb said kindly. "But nonetheless, it was a threat you made. And that's against the law."

Ivan's mom had turned those poison eyes on Ivan. It was probably news to her that her son was a racist bully. I wondered if she saw the photo he put up. I doubted it.

"I understand," I said to Ms. Robb.

She called my mom, and my mom came to get me. Ms. Robb talked to her about my punishment: one week of suspension. The police officer filed a report, but she didn't take me to the station. Because I didn't have a weapon, she agreed the suspension was enough—especially since Ivan's mom suddenly lost interest in persecuting me. When we got home, Mom sent me to my room.

"I don't know what to think right now," she said. "I will figure out your punishment by tomorrow. Meantime, I don't want to see you."

So I lay on my bed and listened to the New York Dolls on my earbuds and tried to go to sleep. But I kept thinking about how hurt my mom looked, like she'd been carved out inside. I'd let her down. She didn't even know why.

CHAPTER EIGHT

The next morning, Mom wanted me to tell her what happened. "What's the story with this photo?" she asked, setting a plate of scrambled eggs and bacon in front of me.

"Just what I told you," I said. "You know how Ivan's been making my life miserable all these years. So I wanted to get back at him. I thought it would be humiliating for him—the dumb picture and everything. And maybe he'd be a little scared."

I poured a big scoop of sugar and a glug of half-and-half into my coffee and stirred it. Then I forked a big mound of eggs into my mouth.

"He was scared, apparently," Mom said. "Congratulations."

"I didn't think it was a big deal," I said.

"I talked with his mom last night, and it was definitely a big deal. He felt quite violated."

"Good."

"Chace," she said, "it's not *good*. You went too far."

"Maybe you wouldn't say that if you saw what he did."

"I was going to ask you about that."

But I didn't want to talk about it. I wasn't going to tell her the whole dumb Muslim bullying story. "What did Ivan's mom tell you?" I asked.

"Not much. Actually, she wanted to know if I could tell *her* anything. She was pretty surprised to hear about Ivan's behavior. Ivan is facing some punishment of his own right now."

"I wish I'd just pressed charges against him instead of retaliating."

"What did he do?" she asked again.

"I don't want to tell you, Mom. You don't want to know."

She took a sip of coffee and sat quietly, waiting me out. But I wasn't going to change my mind. After a while, she set the coffee down. "Okay," she said. "You don't have to tell me."

She picked up her plate and brought it to the dishwasher. I knew what was coming next: it was time to talk about my punishment.

Mom leaned back against the counter and looked at me. "Ella will be staying with your dad next week while we go up north to Tahir's family's land." She explained that we'd be spending the next week clearing the area so they could begin construction on a cabin this summer.

"No way," I said. "I didn't commit murder. I shouldn't have to do forced labor!"

"Unfortunately for you," she said, "I'm still your mom, you still live in my house, and you still follow my rules."

"Come on!" I said. "Why not just ground me or something?"

"Pack plenty of extra socks in case you get wet," she said. "We leave tomorrow before lunch." And then she left the room. Apparently we were done talking about it.

I was so mad I took Mom's car without asking and drove over to see Dad.

"Do you know about this?" I asked him when he answered the door. "How about if I stay with you instead? I mean, she can't make me do this."

Dad stood in the doorway looking at me for a second, not letting me inside. He was wearing running shorts and running shoes. He had never been a runner before, but he'd changed lots of things about himself since he moved out of our house, like growing a beard and playing a lot of rock on his stereo. "She can, and you will do what she says," Dad said. "I actually think it's a good idea."

I pushed past him into the apartment and

collapsed onto the couch. "So you heard what happened?"

"I did. And I think the punishment fits the crime. What you did is serious, and besides, it will be really good for you to do something nice for Tahir."

"You sound like you *like* him," I said.

"He's a good man," Dad replied. I just stared at him in disbelief. "He *is*," Dad said.

"How do you know?" It wasn't that I thought he was a *bad* guy. It was just that I was really struggling with Tahir being in her life, and I assumed my dad would struggle with it too.

"I talked to him once," Dad said.

"You talked to him *once*, and you know he's a good guy. Right."

"All right," Dad said, "I don't know. Maybe he barbecues puppies and robs old ladies. But I doubt it, knowing your mom. She's pretty good about choosing men."

"Well, I don't care," I said. "I don't want to

work myself to death all week on some dude's land. I mean seriously, who does he think he is?"

"Sounds like this was all your mom's idea, not his. And it sounds like you need to show a little more respect to both of them."

I made a spitting sound, like *chuh.*

"You want my advice? You get back in that car, go home, and keep your nose clean. Work hard all week. Act like you actually regret what you did. Act like you actually want to help. Stop being such a baby, Chace. It's time to grow up."

"Okay, okay," I said.

Dad said he was about to take a run. "So, unless you have any other issues to talk about, I'm going to head out."

"There is one other thing," I said. "Jon Sadusky says hi. I was over there the other day, and it was fun chatting with him. I missed the days when you, he, Ollie, and I used to hang out. We were thinking the four of us should do something some time."

Dad tipped his head like he was remembering those good times too. "That's a great idea," he said. "I'll give him a call. Let's plan something for after you serve your time."

Just then my phone buzzed with a text. It was Mom, wondering where I was.

"I better go," I said.

CHAPTER NINE

Tahir had set up a little trailer camper for me, him, and Mom to crash in. Other than sleeping, we spent just about all of our time outside. When I got that headache on Monday, I took a short break in the shade of the trailer. Tahir came over to check on me and got me a big glass of water and a couple of ibuprofens out of the trailer.

"How you doing, buddy?" he said.

Buddy. Oh, boy.

"I'm okay," I said. "I just need a few minutes."

"Take as much time as you need."

He went back down the slope and fired up the chain saw again. I listened to the saw's *rrrrt, rrrrt, rrrrt* as it slipped through the narrow stalks of saplings. Mom ran the big old brush cutter through the sumac again, and I shut my eyes. A few minutes later, I heard the brush cutter turn off and Mom's footsteps coming my way through the leaves. I got up.

"I'm ready," I said before she had time to holler at me. "I'm ready. I'm coming."

It was too soon for the ibuprofen to have kicked in, but I decided that I'd take Dad's advice and work hard. As long as I was going to be here, I might as well accomplish something.

I headed back to my spot and began prying out rocks. Clanged them into the truck. Soon Tahir put the chain saw up by the trailer and came over to help me. I imagined someone purposely collecting a million rocks and planting them here. We had that many to pick up. Some were so big we had to lift them together. But we made some progress. By dinner, we'd cleared a big swath at the end of the driveway where the patio and garden were going to be.

That night we sat down at a picnic table just above the area we'd cleared. Tahir fired up a charcoal grill and cooked us a bunch of chicken thighs he'd been marinating all day. We passed around flatbread and a green salad too.

With the trees Tahir had downed that day, we had a decent view of the lake at sunset. It was maybe the best dinner I'd ever had in my life. Even though we weren't clearing space for *my* cabin and I didn't know if Tahir would stick around with Mom long enough for me to be inside the place, I started to get excited about the project.

The next day, I woke up with a sore back, sore hamstrings, and sore forearms from grabbing and lifting all those rocks. I took more ibuprofen, and that day I got to run the brush cutter. Working the machine was cool, and I didn't have to clear any rocks.

After an hour of mowing the eight-foot-high sumac, we took a break to run a long tape measure up from the edge of the water. By rule from the Department of Natural Resources, you have to set your house at least a hundred feet back from the "ordinary high-water mark." You know, to protect the wetlands, preserve animal habitats, and prevent erosion.

Tahir measured the distance a few different times that day and later in the week, always calculating things like where the porch would begin and where the kitchen windows would be and stuff like that. He drove stakes into the ground here and there with pink ribbons fluttering off them.

We started a couple different burn piles too, with all the trees and saplings and old leaves. Tahir poured gasoline over the piles and let them burn all day. In addition to getting rid of the wood and brush, the burn also helped keep the mosquitoes at bay.

My favorite part was Thursday, when we trimmed trees at the edge of the water access with a boom saw—this long pole with a chain saw attached to the end. Tahir let me do this job, which was a lot of fun. He wanted to leave these nice, towering pines at the edges of his beach, but he didn't want the low branches obstructing the view or the water access. I ran the saw through the branches, and the sawdust and pine needles flew down toward me and settled on my goggles. When we were done, we hauled all the branches up to one of the burn piles.

By that night, we'd mostly cleared the area, but I could tell we wouldn't finish the job that week. A crew was coming with heavy equipment the following week to dig the hole for the foundation, but Tahir wasn't worried. We had created plenty of space for the trucks and tractors to get in, and we'd opened up the area for the foundation as well as the patio, garden, yard, and beach.

We drove into a small town nearby to have pizza for dinner. Mom and Tahir shared a pitcher of beer, and they leaned back with their arms dangling over the chair backs. They laughed a lot and held hands.

Tahir had brought his laptop to the restaurant, and he brought up the blueprints for the cabin to show me. He even had some artist sketches—all sorts of different perspectives of what the cabin would look like. One picture suggested the view out the kitchen window. Another one suggested what the patio would look like. It was going to be a great place to sit and catch more of those sunsets.

Tahir clicked to another picture. "This will be your room when you come up," he said. "It's blue in the picture, but you can choose the paint color."

It looked really nice—you could look out the window and see right to the water. My stomach unknotted a little bit. A tiny bit of that anger disappeared. I was really touched that he'd thought about me with the room.

"How long will it take?" I asked.

"The whole project? We'll be able to sleep in it by early September if everything goes right. If we don't get too much rain and we can work most of the days. We'll still be finishing up things like the landscaping for another year or so."

A big family, with grandparents and little kids, was sitting at a nearby table. The kids were running around the room hollering. They came by and bumped the back of my chair, and their mom told them to be careful. The grandmother grabbed the little girl into a big hug and told her she was "a real terror." Seeing the different generations reminded me of Tahir's story about getting out of Iran when he was a kid. He said he left grandparents and other family members behind.

"Tahir," I said, "you said this is your family cabin, but I haven't seen your parents here all week."

"My parents are older. They wouldn't be much help. I invited them up to see our progress, but they said they would wait until it's done."

"And you don't have any siblings?" I asked.

"None," he said.

"I'd like to help build this cabin," I said suddenly. I hadn't planned to say it, but once I did, I knew it was true. Now that I'd started, I wanted to be a part of finishing this project. I had never done anything really big before.

Mom and Tahir looked at me with dumbstruck expressions.

"What?" I said. "I would. I could learn a lot! You told me you're going to wire and hang lights—you could teach me to do that. You're going to need help staining the siding and sanding the wood floors and hooking up appliances and, I don't know, lots of stuff. Right?"

"I guess that's right," Tahir said.

"And school's almost out for the summer. I'll have free time."

"I thought you were going to get a job," Mom said. "We talked about that."

"Yeah, I know," I said, deflated.

"Well, I could pay you for your help," Tahir said. "That would only be fair."

"No, Tahir," Mom said. "You don't have to do that."

"Carol, please," he said. "I'd like to. I'd have to hire help anyway."

Mom studied me. "You really want to do that?" she asked.

"I do," I said.

And so it was settled.

CHAPTER TEN

On Friday, we didn't work very hard. Tahir and I burned some more brush and branches, and we cleared more rocks and weeds from the spot where the water access would be. But after lunch, we packed up our stuff and drove home. I slept about thirty hours over the weekend, but I felt great. My arms were stronger, and my outlook was more positive than it had been in months. Years, maybe. I couldn't remember feeling so good.

Doing a hard job, seeing the results take form right before my eyes—not to mention learning skills like how to run a boom saw, drive the little Bobcat, and even spray for poison ivy—all these things made me feel competent. Clearing that land helped me clear out the anger too. There was just one more big rock that I wanted to pry out.

Monday in health class, Ivan didn't look at me. But Toua was definitely giving me stares. He was glaring at me like he wanted to burn me alive. In gym class, we did these fitness tests called the pacer, so we didn't interact at all.

After classes ended, I saw Christa in the hall. I felt like I wanted to tell her something, but I wasn't sure what. So I just said, "You were right about those Instagram photos. It was mean."

"Yeah," she said, but she didn't seem mad or anything. She actually stood there with me for a while, which was unusual. She was really cute, and cute girls never wanted to hang with me. She told me that her family and Ivan's family were friends, just like my family and

Ollie's were. I guess that's why she was more sensitive about the mean stuff that people were saying about Ivan. The stuff *I* was saying. "Did you hear? His mom is the one who reported that threat, not Ivan!"

"Really?"

"Totally! She's a real b-word!"

Just then I spotted Ivan and Toua heading toward the schools front exits. "Hey," I said to Christa, "I gotta run!"

"Bye!" she said.

When I got outside, I scanned the parking lot until I saw them walking toward the road.

"Hey, Ivan!" I called.

He turned to look at me. So did Toua.

"What do you want?" Toua said when I caught up to them.

"I want to talk to Ivan," I said. Toua didn't go anywhere, so I went ahead and started. I said, "Hey, Ivan, I just wanted to say I'm sorry. That was pretty creepy of me to post that photo. It was a crappy thing to do."

"No kidding," Toua said. But I didn't even look at him. Ivan was staring at me with those dark eyes, only now I didn't hate him so much. He was just a kid, dealing with the jagged landscape of his life, just like I was.

"Anyway," I said to him, "I'm sorry."

Neither of them said anything to that. Ivan looked at me like I was from Mars or something. I didn't care. I gave him a good pat on the shoulder, put my earbuds in, and said, "See ya, man." Then I hit Play on the Ramones' *Rocket to Russia* and walked home.

ABOUT THE AUTHOR

Herman Brown is a writer from Minneapolis.

SUSPENDED

THE CONFESSIONAL

A CUT TOO FAR

HIGH DRAMA

OVER THE TRACKS

TESTING THE TRUTH